NATURAL WONDERS

Victoria Falls

One of the World's Most Spectacular Waterfalls

Anna Rebus

WEIGL PUBLISHERS INC.

Published by Weigl Publishers Inc.
350 5th Avenue, Suite 3304, PMB 6G
New York, NY 10118-0069

Website: www.weigl.com

Library of Congress Cataloging-in-Publication Data

Rebus, Anna.
  Victoria Falls : one of the world's most spectacular waterfalls / Anna Rebus.
     p. cm. -- (Natural wonders)
  Includes index.
  ISBN 1-59036-453-8 (library binding : alk. paper) -- ISBN 1-59036-459-7 (soft cover : alk. paper)
  1. Victoria Falls (Zambia and Zimbabwe)--Juvenile literature. I. Title. II. Series: Natural wonders (Weigl Publishers)
  DT3140.V54R43 2007
  968.91--dc22
                      2006015264

Printed in the United States of America
1 2 3 4 5 6 7 8 9 0 08 07 06 05 04

Editor
Heather Kissock

Design
Terry Paulhus

Photograph Credits

Every reasonable effort has been made to trace ownership and to obtain permission to reprint copyright material. The publishers would be pleased to have any errors or omissions brought to their attention so that they may be corrected in subsequent printings.

Cover: The Victoria Falls are fed by the Zambezi River. Through the power of erosion, the Zambezi River carved through rock to create the falls.

All of the Internet URLs given in the book were valid at the time of publication. However, due to the dynamic nature of the Internet, some addresses may have changed, or sites may have ceased to exist since publication. While the author and publisher regret any inconvenience this may cause readers, no responsibility for any such changes can be accepted by either the author or the publisher.

Contents

A Wealth of Life

At more than 5,580 feet (1,700 meters) wide and 355 feet (108 m) high, Victoria Falls in southern Africa is the largest curtain of falling water in the world. It is so large that at times the spray from the falls rises to a height of 1,200 feet (365 m) and is visible 25 miles (40 kilometers) away.

A wealth of plants and animals live in the Victoria Falls area. Some of the land on either side of the falls is preserved as national parks. Many large mammals live in the parks, including rare white rhinoceroses, cheetahs, hippopotamuses, wildebeests, and elephants. Smaller animals include birds, otters, wild dogs, and warthogs. There are also many species of plants. Some of these plants can be eaten, while others are used as medicine.

Visitors from around the world view the spectacular falls and go on safari to see the wildlife of the surrounding region.

Victoria Falls Facts

- Victoria Falls is one-and-a-half times as wide and twice as high as North America's Niagara Falls.

- Victoria Falls is on the Zambezi River in southern Africa.

- The Zambezi River is about 1,600 miles (2,735 km) long and is the fourth longest river in Africa.

- Between February and April each year, the Zambezi River is in full flood. Every minute, about 110 million gallons (500 million liters) of water flow over Victoria Falls.

- The locals call Victoria Falls *Mosi-Oa-Tunya*, or "the smoke that thunders."

- In November, the water level of the Zambezi River is low. About 2.64 million gallons (10 million liters) of water flow over the falls each minute.

Victoria Falls Locator

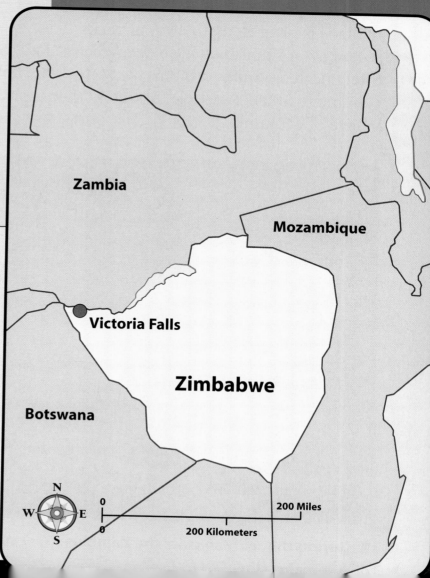

Where in the World?

Victoria Falls is located on the Zambezi River, which forms a natural border between the countries of Zambia and Zimbabwe. The Zambezi River also flows through Angola, Namibia, Botswana, and Mozambique. Along the way, smaller rivers feed into the Zambezi. During the rainy season between November and March, massive amounts of water flow along the mighty Zambezi.

Directly opposite Victoria Falls is a lush forest. Some of the land near the falls is protected as national parks. The falls and national parks are so important that they have been declared a **UNESCO World Heritage Site**. Located 6 miles (10 km) away from the falls, the town of Livingstone is home to 100,000 people. About 8,000 people live in the nearby traditional village of Mukuni.

■ **During the rainy season, the Zambezi River swells in size. However, the water flow remains slow.**

Puzzler

Victoria Falls is on the Zambezi River in Africa. This river flows through six countries before reaching the Indian Ocean.

Q Where are these countries located? Find each one on the map. Also find the Indian Ocean.

Angola	Zambia
Botswana	Zimbabwe
Mozambique	Indian Ocean
Namibia	

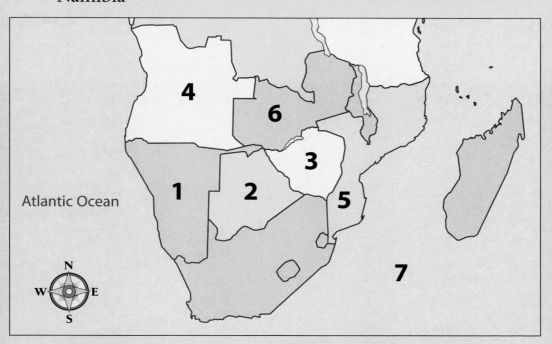

 1. Namibia 2. Botswana 3. Zimbabwe 4. Angola 5. Mozambique 6. Zambia 7. Indian Ocean

A Trip Back in Time

The region around Victoria Falls began to form millions of years ago. The falls themselves are a result of volcanic activity, erosion, and the flow of the Zambezi River.

The Victoria Falls area stands on a volcanic layer of rock called basalt. Millions of years ago, a vast inland sea covered what is today the northern part of Botswana. As the sea water levels went down, fine **sediments** were deposited on top of the basalt. The Zambezi River has slowly cut its way through the layers of basalt and sediments. From the air above the falls a series of cracks in the land can be seen. This shows that the river has changed its course through time.

The Zambezi River continues to shape the land to this day. Above the falls, the river is wide and flows around islands. It then plunges over the falls into a series of deep **gorges**.

▬ **The Zambezi River supports many types of vegetation. Grasses, Rhodesian teak, and ferns grow along the river.**

The Running River

The Zambezi River is divided into upper, middle, and lower river sections. Victoria Falls marks the boundary between the upper and middle Zambezi.

The Upper River: The Zambezi River has its **source** in the country of Zambia. In this section, the river is joined by many smaller rivers, or tributaries. The river becomes wider as more water from these tributaries flows into it.

The Middle River: After the water plunges over Victoria Falls, the river runs for around 150 miles (240 km). Two dams have been built on the middle river that generate **hydroelectric** power. Kariba Dam was completed in 1959. Cahora Bassa Dam opened in 1974. Each dam has created a reservoir, or lake.

The Lower River: From Cahora Bassa Dam, the Zambezi River makes its way to the Indian Ocean. This section of the river is about 400 miles (650 km) long. The delta of the Zambezi is where the river meets the ocean.

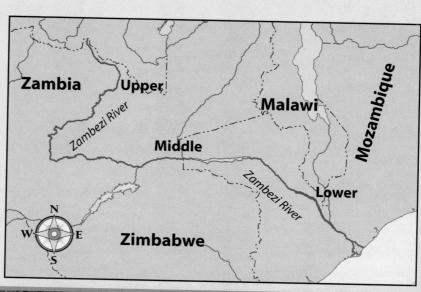

Plentiful Plants

A cloud of mist is produced as water plunges over Victoria Falls. The mist has created a rain forest opposite the falls, where ebony, mahogany, and fig trees grow. This forest remains lush even when the surrounding countryside is very dry.

A number of important plant **species** are found around Victoria Falls. One of these, the tree fern, grows throughout southern Africa. It usually reaches heights of between 6.5 and 10 feet (2 and 3 m). Some tree ferns can grow up to 26 feet (8 m) tall. Scientists believe that the tree fern could become rare in the wild.

Not all plants at Victoria Falls have been there for long. Some have been brought to the Victoria Falls area by early European settlers. Many have become pest plants. Lantana is a pretty plant, but it spreads quickly and poisons cattle.

■ **Lantana flowers attract butterflies, and their fruits are eaten and dispersed by many animals. The lantana has become widespread in tropical areas.**

The Rainy Season

The volume of water in the Zambezi River changes throughout the seasons. This region experiences rainy and dry seasons every year.

The rainy season occurs between November and March when the weather becomes very hot and humid. Between February and April, the Zambezi River is in full flood. There is so much spray rising up from Victoria Falls that it can be difficult to get a good view of the falls from the ground. During the rainy season, storms form suddenly and are followed quickly by sunshine and blue skies.

The dry season occurs between April and October. By September and October, there is much less water going over the falls and much less spray. Visitors can clearly see the cliff edge that the water plunges over.

Spray from the falls rises in the air. In sunny weather, it often produces rainbows.

Zambezi Animals

Some amazing animals live near Victoria Falls. Large mammals, such as lions, elephants, zebras, giraffes, and rhinoceroses, roam across the land. Grazing animals, such as antelopes and impalas, must keep a careful eye out for hunting cheetahs. These big cats are the fastest mammals on Earth.

More than 400 species of bird live in the Victoria Falls area. The Zambezi River Basin, of which Victoria Falls is part, is home to 95 percent of the world's wattled cranes. Fewer than 10,000 wattled cranes remain in southern Africa.

Scientists have found 84 species of fish in the waters above the falls, while 39 species of fish have been recorded below the falls. Some fish are very large. The giant vundu is a type of catfish. It can grow to more than 6 feet (1.8 m) long and weigh up to 132 pounds (60 kilograms).

Wattled cranes are tall, long-legged birds that use their powerful bill to grasp fish, amphibians, and other small animals that live in water.

Endangered Species

In southern Africa, many plants and animal species are in danger of becoming extinct. This means that a certain species no longer exists. Humans are often to blame for plant and animal extinctions. People need places to live, but in the process of building homes, they destroy important **habitat**. Along the Zambezi River, dams have been built. As a result, some habitats have been flooded, while others have dried out.

Zambia once had a large population of rhinoceroses, but they were hunted by **poachers** to near extinction for their horns. A few white rhinoceroses have been brought from other countries into Mosi-Oa-Tunya National Park near Victoria Falls. However, some of them have died. Poachers have also hunted elephants for their tusks. Some herds of elephants and rhinoceroses are now guarded by rangers.

■ A white rhinoceros's nose horn is made from a hairlike substance. The horn never stops growing, and if broken off, it will grow back.

Researching the Falls

Scientists study Victoria Falls in different ways. Studying water samples taken from the falls area tells scientists if pollution is entering the river farther upstream. Photographs of the falls taken from an airplane can help researchers understand how the rocks have eroded over time.

Scientists know that Victoria Falls, the Zambezi River, and the surrounding land exist in a delicate balance. The survival of local plants and animals and their habitats can be affected by drought, floods, fire, and human settlement. Two large hydroelectric dams have been built along the Zambezi River. While they provide power for people, dams upset the normal flow of water. Researchers study how the dams have affected the natural environment.

From the air, visitors can see how the landscape around Victoria Falls has been shaped by the water.

Biography

David Livingstone (1813–1873)

David Livingstone devoted much of his life to exploring the continent of Africa. Livingstone was a doctor and missionary turned explorer. He traveled 29,000 miles (47,000 km) in Africa. In 1855, he became the first European to see and describe Victoria Falls, which he named after Queen Victoria of Great Britain.

In 1866, Livingstone set out to find the source of Africa's Nile River. Having no contact with the outside world for several years, Livingstone was feared dead. Henry Stanley, a journalist for the *New York Herald* was sent to find Livingstone. Stanley reached Livingstone in November 1871 and uttered the now famous phrase "Dr. Livingstone, I presume?"

Located near Victoria Falls, the town of Livingstone, Zambia, is named after this great explorer.

Facts of Life

Born: March 19, 1813

Hometown: Blantyre, South Lanarkshire, Scotland

Occupation: Doctor, Missionary, Explorer

Died: May 1, 1873

The Big Picture

The Zambezi River is one of many great river systems found throughout the world. Rivers provide important habitats for animals. Towns and cities are often built near rivers. People use rivers as a source of drinking water and food, as transportation routes, as a place for leisure activities, and to generate hydroelectricity.

ARCTIC OCEAN

Mackenzie River

NORTH AMERICA

Mississippi River

St.Lawrence River

ATLANTIC OCEAN

PACIFIC OCEAN

Amazon River

SOUTH AMERICA

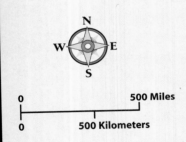

Map Legend	
Amazon River	4,000 miles (6,437 km)
Danube River	1,770 miles (2,850 km)
Ganges River	1,560 miles (2,510 km)
Mackenzie River	1,120 miles (1,800 km)
Mississippi River	2,340 miles (3,766 km)
Murray River	1,609 miles (2,589 km)
Nile River	4,160 miles (6,695 km)
St. Lawrence River	800 miles (1,300 km)
Yangtze (Chang) River	3,900 miles (6,276 km)

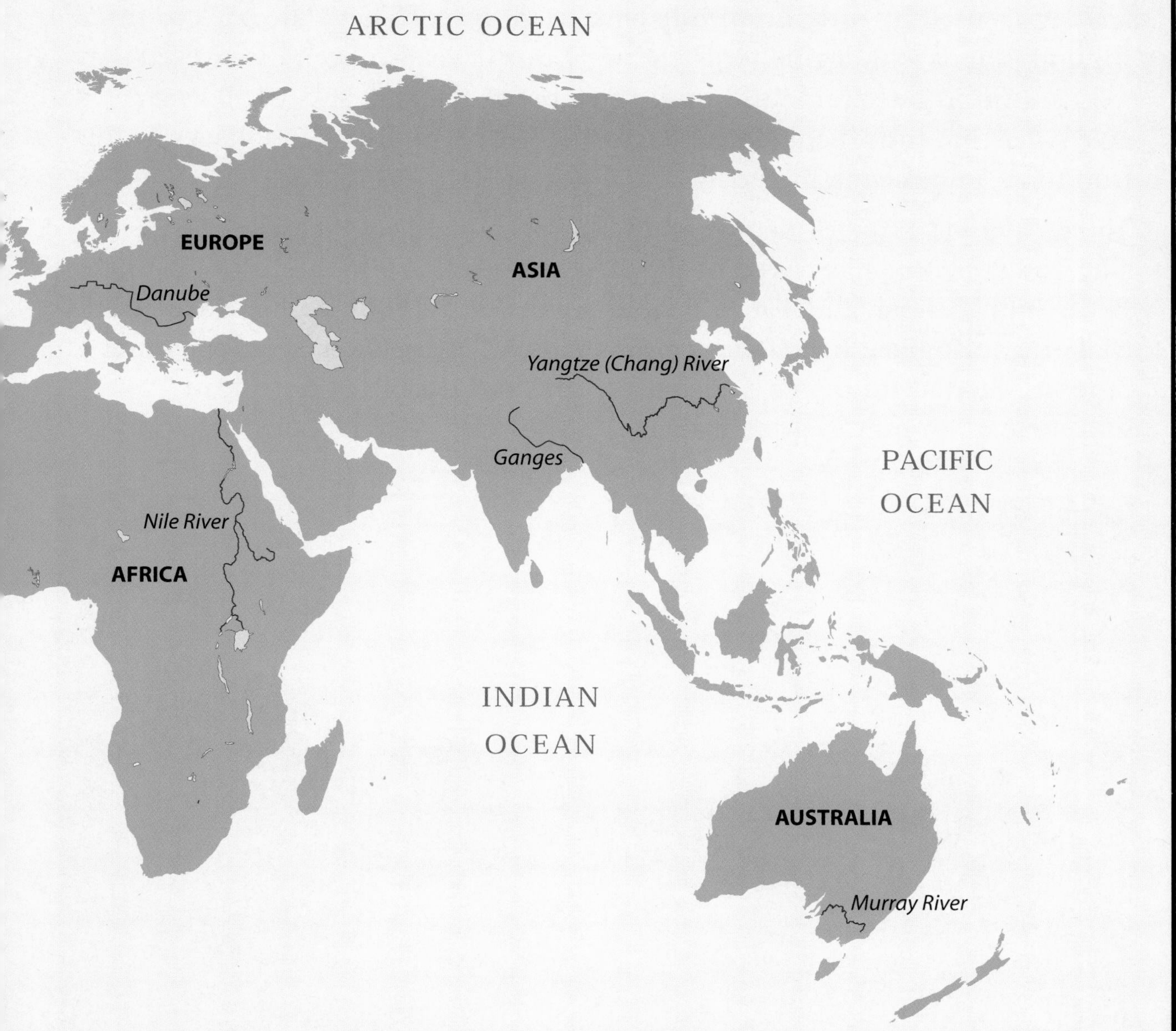

ARCTIC OCEAN

EUROPE

ASIA

Danube

Yangtze (Chang) River

Ganges

PACIFIC
OCEAN

Nile River

AFRICA

INDIAN
OCEAN

AUSTRALIA

Murray River

People of the Falls

People have lived in the Victoria Falls area for a very long time. Stone tools used by early **hominids** have been found. They date back to three million years ago. Digging tools and weapons have also been discovered that tell us **hunter-gatherers** lived in the area between 2,000 and 10,000 years ago. After that time, people near Victoria Falls began living in villages, using iron tools, and raising livestock.

Today, there is a mix of people and cultures living near Victoria Falls. The Tonga people have lived in the area for at least 700 years, along with Leya, Subiya, Toka, and Totela people. By the mid-1800s, a people called the Makololo also lived here. They called the falls "Mosi-Oa-Tunya," meaning "the smoke that thunders." Ndebele people and people of European **ancestry** are more recent arrivals.

◼ **Local people use dugout canoes to catch fish in the Zambezi River.**

Puzzler

Baobab trees grow near Victoria Falls. The baobab is an unusual tree. It only has leaves for three months of the year. During the other nine months, it stores water in its thick trunk. Baobab trees grow in many other places, too.

Q In which parts of the world do baobab trees grown?

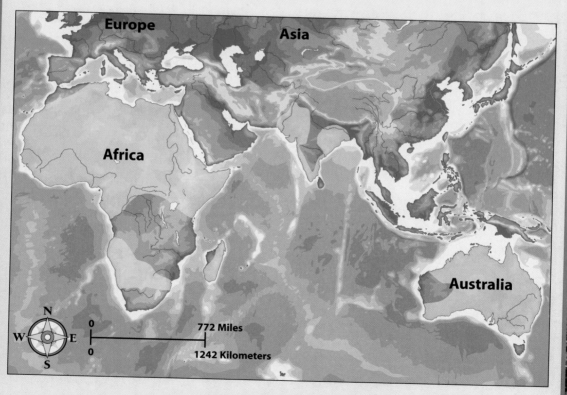

Europe

Asia

Africa

Australia

N
W — E
S

0
0
772 Miles
1242 Kilometers

A Baobab trees grow in the savannas, or tropical grasslands, of Africa (including Madagascar), India, and Australia. These savannas are mostly near the equator.

Local Knowledge

Over thousands of years, people living near Victoria Falls have gathered knowledge about local plants. They know which species are poisonous and which are safe to eat.

A plant may be useful in many different ways. Various parts of the baobab tree have different uses. The inner bark is made into a strong rope. The seedpods are used to carry liquids. The fruit pulp is mixed with water to create a refreshing drink. Young leaves are used in soups, and the seeds can be roasted and eaten.

Some plants can also be used to treat ailments, including skin irritations and stomach upsets. The leaves, roots, and bark of the African ebony and Cape fig trees are used in traditional medicine. The fruits and leaves of the Cape fig are also given to cattle to make them produce more milk.

The people of the Zambezi River Valley have been using plants for food and medicine for many years. Some plants can be turned into grain and cooked.

Sacred Ceremony

Located near Victoria Falls, Mukuni Village is home to 8,000 people. Mukuni villagers belong to the Toka-Leya culture. Victoria Falls is an important and sacred place for the Toka-Leya people. They believe that the spirits of their ancestors dwell around the falls. Each year before the rains come, the Lwiindi ceremony is performed in a hut near the village graveyard. A sacred drum is played, and villagers pray to their ancestors to make the rains come. After the ceremony, the villagers feast, dance, and sing.

It is the duty of the Bedyango, or a Toka-Leya high priestess, to pray for rain during the Lwiindi ceremony.

Natural Attractions

Each year, more than a million tourists visit Victoria Falls. Tourists spend money on food, hotels, and souvenirs. This money helps to support the local community and provides people with jobs.

Tourists can view the falls in different ways. Just below the falls, the Victoria Falls Bridge carries trains, cars, and foot traffic. Some people take flights over the falls in helicopters or small planes. A series of walking trails allows visitors to get so close to the falls they get wet from the spray. In the park around the falls, visitors can go on **safari** and get a close-up view of animals such as lions, elephants, rhinoceroses, and zebras in their natural habitat.

■ **Many people enjoy whitewater rafting and canoeing on the Zambezi River. Others bungee jump off the Victoria Falls Bridge.**

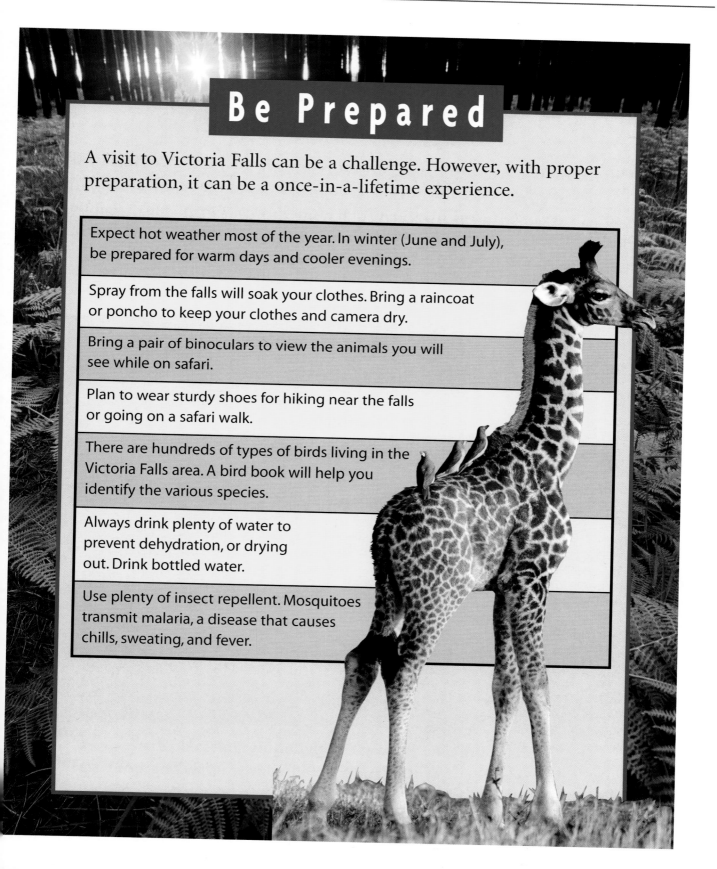

Be Prepared

A visit to Victoria Falls can be a challenge. However, with proper preparation, it can be a once-in-a-lifetime experience.

Expect hot weather most of the year. In winter (June and July), be prepared for warm days and cooler evenings.

Spray from the falls will soak your clothes. Bring a raincoat or poncho to keep your clothes and camera dry.

Bring a pair of binoculars to view the animals you will see while on safari.

Plan to wear sturdy shoes for hiking near the falls or going on a safari walk.

There are hundreds of types of birds living in the Victoria Falls area. A bird book will help you identify the various species.

Always drink plenty of water to prevent dehydration, or drying out. Drink bottled water.

Use plenty of insect repellent. Mosquitoes transmit malaria, a disease that causes chills, sweating, and fever.

Disappearing Habitat

People travel from all over the world to see the spectacular Victoria Falls. Visitors need hotels to stay in, roads to travel on, and activities to do. All of this development means the land is no longer left in its natural state. Once another road or hotel is built, animals can no longer roam free in that area. On the other hand, visitors spend money that helps support the local economy and provide people with jobs.

■ **Thousands of tourists who view the falls stay in hotels, such as the Victoria Falls Hotel.**

Finding a balance between promoting tourism and protecting the environment is very difficult. More visitors mean more land is cleared for development. Habitat is lost, and some animals in this area have become endangered. Land on either side of Victoria Falls has been protected from development by being declared a national park.

Should more development be allowed at Victoria Falls?

YES	NO
Tourism gives local people jobs and money. People can buy homes and send their children to school.	 More development will mean there is less habitat for animals.
More roads and hotels mean more people can experience the beauty of the falls.	Visitors create pollution, use precious natural resources, and leave behind garbage.
Land can be set aside as national parks where development can be controlled. 	Some of the hotels and shops are not owned by people in the local area. The money the owners make does not go back into the local economy.

Timeline

3 million years ago
Hominids, the ancestors of early humans, live near Victoria Falls.

2,000–10,000 years ago
Hunter-gatherers live in the Victoria Falls area.

2,000 years ago
People begin living in villages near Victoria Falls. They use iron tools and keep livestock.

1200s
The village of Gundu is founded near Victoria Falls. It is later renamed Mukuni village.

1855
David Livingstone is the first European to see and describe Victoria Falls.

1862
Thomas Baines is the first European to paint a picture of Victoria Falls.

British politician and businessman Cecil Rhodes (1853–1902) commissioned the building of a rail bridge over Victoria Falls. It was completed in 1905.

A hippopotamus in the Zambezi River calls and displays to defend his territory from other hippopotamuses.

1900
Cecil Rhodes commissions the building of Victoria Falls Bridge.

1903
The first prehistoric hand ax is found at Victoria Falls.

1905
The Victoria Falls Bridge is opened.

1935
The capital of Zambia is moved from Livingstone, near Victoria Falls, to Lusaka.

Elephants drink from the Zambezi River at Mana Pools in Zimbabwe.

Steam locomotives cross the Victoria Falls Bridge, which was rebuilt in 1930 to carry road traffic as well as the railroad.

1972
Victoria Falls becomes a national park 38 years after it was first made a protected area.

1989
Mosi-Oa-Tunya and Victoria Falls National Park are listed as a UNESCO World Heritage Site.

1990
African elephants are officially listed as an endangered species. This makes it against the law to trade in elephant ivory products.

2003
Two white rhinoceroses die at Mosi-Oa-Tunya National Park near Victoria Falls. This leaves only three white rhinoceroses in all of Zambia.

1955-1959
Kariba Dam is constructed on the Zambezi River.

1964
Rhodesia, previously governed by Great Britain, becomes independent and is renamed Zambia.

1969-1974
Construction of the Cahora Bassa Dam on the Zambezi River takes place.

What Have You Learned?

True or False?

Decide whether the following statements are true or false. If the statement is false, make it true.

1. In 1755, David Livingstone became the first European to see Victoria Falls.

2. Victoria Falls is the largest curtain of falling water in the world.

3. Elephants are hunted by poachers for their hide.

4. The spray from Victoria Falls can be seen 250 miles (400 km) away.

ANSWERS

1. False. He saw the falls in 1855.
2. True.
3. False. Elephants are killed for their ivory tusks.
4. False. The spray can be seen up to 25 miles (40 km) away.

Short Answer

Answer the following questions using information from the book.

1. Victoria Falls is found on the border of which two countries?

2. The Zambezi River flows through which countries?

3. What is the name of the ceremony performed at Mukuni village to make the rains come?

4. How long is the Zambezi River?

5. Victoria Falls is what type of UNESCO site?

ANSWERS

1. Zambia and Zimbabwe
2. Angola, Namibia, Botswana, Zambia, Zimbabwe, and Mozambique
3. Lwiindi ceremony
4. about 1,600 miles (2,735 km) long
5. World Heritage Site

Multiple Choice

Choose the best answer for the following questions.

1. The local name for Victoria Falls, "Mosi-Oa-Tunya," means:
   a) "The mist that is wet"
   b) "The smoke that thunders"
   c) "The falling water"
   d) "The river falls away"

2. Which cultural group lives at Mukuni Village near Victoria Falls?
   a) The Cree
   b) The Hopi
   c) The Inca
   d) The Toka-Leya

3. One of the two dams on the Zambezi River is called the Cahora Bassa Dam. What is the other one called?
   a) The Hoover Dam
   b) The Aswan High Dam
   c) The Kariba Dam
   d) The Three Gorges Dam

4. When the last member of a species dies, it is said to be:
   a) Rare
   b) Abundant
   c) Threatened
   d) Extinct

ANSWERS
1. b
2. d
3. c
4. d

Find Out for Yourself

Books

Ayo, Yvonne. *Africa*. DK Eyewitness Guides, 2000.

Holmes, Tim. *Zambia*. Cultures of the World Series. New York: Marshall Cavendish, 1998.

Rogers, Barbara Radcliffe and Stillman D. Rogers. *Zimbabwe*. Enchantment of the World Series. New York: Children's Press, 2002.

Websites

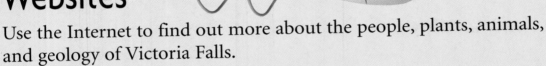

Use the Internet to find out more about the people, plants, animals, and geology of Victoria Falls.

African Wildlife Foundation
www.awf.org
Learn about the animals that live in southern Africa and the projects that are helping to protect them.

Exploring Africa
http://exploringafrica.matrix.mus.edu
On this site you can learn about the culture, history, and people of Africa.

Google Images
http://images.google.com
Visit this site to view thousands of photos of Victoria Falls and the people, animals, and places near the falls.

Skill Matching Page

What did you learn? Look at the questions in the "Skills" column. Compare them to the page number of the answers in the "Page" column. Refresh your memory by reading the "Answer" column below.

SKILLS	ANSWER	PAGE
What facts did I learn from this book?	I learned that Victoria Falls is the largest curtain of falling water in the world.	4
What skills did I learn?	I learned how to read maps.	7, 9, 16-17
What activities did I do?	I answered the questions in the quiz.	28–29
How can I find out more?	I can read the books and visit the websites from the Find Out for Yourself page.	30
How can I get involved?	I can help save endangered species by supporting organizations like the African Wildlife Foundation.	30

Glossary

ancestry: people from the past who are related to people today
gorges: narrow and deep passages that cut through rock
habitat: the environment where a plant or animal is normally found
hominids: the ancient ancestors of humans
hunter-gatherers: people that survive by hunting for animals and collecting plants to eat
hydroelectricity: electricity that is created by the flow of running water
poachers: people who illegally hunt animals
safari: a trip that people take to view animals in their natural environment
sediments: silt and sand that is carried or deposited by a flowing river or body of water
source: the place where a river starts
species: a specific group of plants or animals that share the same characteristics
UNESCO World Heritage Site: a place that is of natural or cultural importance to the entire world. UNESCO is an abbreviation for United Nations Educational, Scientific, and Cultural Organization.

Index